1

Fish Tank

A Light-Hearted, One-Act Comedy

by Lowery Christopher Collins

Fish Tank

A Light-Hearted, One-Act Comedy

BY LOWERY CHRISTOPHER COLLINS

Ponderlake Publishing

FISH TANK,
A LIGHT-HEARTED, ONE-ACT COMEDY

Written by Lowery Christopher Collins

Copyright © 2020 by Lowery Christopher Collins

Ponderlake Publishing: www.ponderlake.com

Playwright and/or Royalty Information: www.ChristopherCollinsOnline.com

ISBN 978-0-9992241-6-8

Fish Tank

A Light-Hearted, One-Act Comedy

by Lowery Christopher Collins

The set is an average living room. In the middle back of the room is an aquarium. Margaret *enters stage right. She is carrying a broom and a dustpan. She proceeds to sweep an area where, evidently, something has either slipped or has been broken. She is a woman in her mid-thirties. She is dressed very conservatively, as if she has been at work.*

As she is sweeping, Allison *enters stage left through a door. About the same age as* Margaret, *she, too, is dressed very professionally, but she is carrying a handbag, evidence that she has been out.*

ALLISON.   The queen is home.

MARGARET. Quit your buzzing and give the drones a hand.

ALLISON.   Margaret, I had no idea that you were home.

MARGARET. I've worked at the same business for the last eight years. I get off work at 4. I always get off work at 4. I'm home by 4:30. I'm always home by 4:30. It's 5 o'clock, and you didn't know that I'd be home?

ALLISON.   Someone's rather *irritable*, isn't she?

MARGARET. Don't even go there.

ALLISON.   It's so fun to be judgmental. Aren't I cute?

MARGARET. It's not becoming. Let other people make stupid comments. It sounds treasonous coming out you.

ALLISON.   Touché. What's your problem, though? You're in a mood.

MARGARET. Allison, I'm trying to clean this mess up.

11

ALLISON.　What happened?

MARGARET.　I dropped the ashtray out on the floor.

ALLISON.　Because . . . *(leading)*

MARGARET.　. . . I wanted to. A new sport. It goes with the wallpaper. A test of the laws of
　　gravity.

ALLISON.　Margaret?

MARGARET.　It was an accident, Allison. An accident. It's pretty obvious.

ALLISON.　What is your deal today?

MARGARET.　My deal? *(calming)* I don't know. I'm just a bit tense. That's all. I even dropped
　　the ashtray on the floor. I never do things like that.

ALLISON.　And you don't smoke anymore.

MARGARET.　I know. But I did this afternoon.

ALLISON.　You stopped three years ago.

MARGARET.　I know.

ALLISON.　Where did you get them? Did you stop and buy them?

MARGARET.　I thought about it, but I remembered that I had some hidden from myself here in
　　the house. I allowed myself to remember where I had them hidden.

ALLISON.　Ah, selective memory. I have used that. Very useful skill.

MARGARET.　Very.

ALLISON.　I still haven't heard the reason for the sudden plunge back into the world of
　　nicotine, yellow teeth, bad breath, and tar-coated lungs.

MARGARET.　You make it sound so glamorous.

ALLISON.　Hey, you puff on the things.

MARGARET.　Did. Well, do. *(Frustrated.)* Aw, I did today. I'll probably hide them in a
　　memorable place for another three years. It's just been a, well, for lack of a bad
　　enough example of profanity, it has been a *bad* day.

ALLISON.　Come. Put the Holly Homemaker stuff away. Come sit. Tell me all about it.

MARGARET.　Holly Homemaker? Where did you get that? I swear, Allison, you take your job
　　way too seriously. It's one thing to write for the public interest. It's quite another
　　to create your own metaphors around me. I have known you too long. I
　　remember when you couldn't spell "cat."

12

ALLISON. You do not.

MARGARET. I most certainly do.

ALLISON. I could always spell. You're the one who . . .

MARGARET. Don't start.

ALLISON. And that wasn't a metaphor.

MARGARET. Allison!

ALLISON. Margaret! *(Grinning.)* Come tell me all about your day.

MARGARET. Why do I suddenly feel like Ricky and David Nelson are going to bound down the stairs and ask, "Mom, what's for dinner?"

ALLISON. We don't have stairs.

MARGARET. True.

ALLISON. How long have we been cousins?

MARGARET. *(Looking at her as if she were insane.)* Um, Allison, dear. We were born that way. Blood kinship is a relation before birth.

ALLISON. My point exactly. A lifetime of trust.

MARGARET. Well . . . *(Sarcastic.)*

ALLISON. *(Emphasizing.)* A LIFETIME OF TRUST! Over ten years of living in the same house. Sharing expenses. Laughing. Talking. Crying. Singing.

MARGARET. Fighting.

ALLISON. That, too. But it goes with the territory. This is taking way too long. It's like a play that won't get on with the plot. *(Pauses, then slowly and deliberately)* What happened today that upset you?

MARGARET. *(Giving up and joining ALLISON on the couch.)* What didn't happen? On the way to work, a ninety-five-year-old kamikaze took out my side mirror at about 120 miles per hour . . .

ALLISON. No!

MARGARET. Yes.

ALLISON. Were you hurt?

MARGARET. No. That's later. He got away. Didn't even know he hit me or just too old to care anymore.

ALLISON. I know the feeling.

MARGARET. What?

ALLISON.   Nothing. Go on, dear.

MARGARET. I stopped to assess the damage. It was there that I must have dropped my wallet.

ALLISON.   No.

MARGARET. Yes. Of course, I didn't realize that until I tried to pay for lunch. But I am ahead of myself. I got to work about thirty minutes late, and lo and behold, there is the new executive director of accounts working his first day—a week early. And I am late. The queen of punctuality—thirty minutes late. My first real day at work with him—and I am late. Late.

ALLISON.   I think we established that.

MARGARET. Okay. And the man's name, and I kid you not. Are you ready?

ALLISON.   Braced and prepared.

MARGARET. Mr. Bumstead.

ALLISON.   No!

MARGARET. Yes.

ALLISON.   No!!

MARGARET. Yes, Sherwood Bumstead.

ALLISON.   *(Laughing.)* You are making this up.

MARGARET. Is this the face, the nicotine-covered face, of someone telling a lie?

ALLISON.   This is too good. This is fiction.

MARGARET. Truth is stranger. Remember? And by the way, I am not through. I get to work thirty minutes late . . .

ALLISON.   I remember.

MARGARET. Yes, and when I finally get to my office, Mildred has mistaken all the Drewry papers for trash and tossed them in the incinerator.

ALLISON.   No.

MARGARET. Yes, three weeks of late-night number crunching up in smoke. And then Bumstead, having heard that I have the account finished and has heard that I am "brilliant" with the numbers, comes in, not in a great mood—he holds punctuality more highly than even I do—anyway, he comes in and asks to see the papers. Mr. Drewry is coming in at 2 to finalize the account.

ALLISON.   Margaret, this is horrible.

14

MARGARET. Stay awhile and be patient, I have more of the story, Gertrude.

ALLISON.   You just called me Gertrude!

MARGARET.   From *Hamlet*.

ALLISON.   I know. I caught the allusion. I'm just impressed.

MARGARET.   Anyway, I have to tell Dagwood, I mean, Mr. Bumstead, that Mildred did the Cheech and Chong bit with the Drewry papers, but I don't think he bought it. He smiled and firmly asked me to have something impressive for Drewry by 2 p.m. I smiled and submitted.

ALLISON.   How unlike you.

MARGARET. I know. Then the mail came.

ALLISON.   A letter bomb?

MARGARET. Close. A postcard from Marcus.

ALLISON.   Oh, no.

MARGARET. Yes, Marcus and Cynthia on their honeymoon in Italy. He sent me a postcard, Allison.

ALLISON.   Tacky. Tacky.

MARGARET. I mean we were engaged for, for . . . a long time.

ALLISON.   Over two years.

MARGARET. Thank you.

ALLISON.   You're welcome.

MARGARET. I could never get him to commit to a wedding date. Then he finds that cheap hussy, and they tie the knot in a month. And *then* they send me a postcard from the very place I've wanted to go all my life.

ALLISON.   That is beyond tacky. That is sorry.

MARGARET. You ain't just whistling "Dixie," darlin'. I was an emotional wreck for an hour after that.

ALLISON.   And then lunch.

MARGARET. Yes, with no money—from earlier. I don't want to get into it. (*Pauses.*) And Ethan Plumber had to pay for my lunch.

ALLISON.   No.

MARGARET. Yes.

ALLISON. Not Ethan. That is bad news. He loves you as it is. Now he feels you owe him a debt.

MARGARET. Again, thank you for your insight.

ALLISON. That was not wise, Margaret. He's not just some little nerd boy. He is a strange character—the kind you can expect to pop up later.

MARGARET. He was in the deli, and I didn't know anyone else there, except Dagwood, I mean Mr. Bumstead, I was sure wasn't going to ask him for a penny.

ALLISON. This is not good.

MARGARET. Let me finish.

ALLISON. There's more?

MARGARET. Yes.

ALLISON. No.

MARGARET. Yes. I frantically work on the Drewry papers before and after and even during lunch. I get them in semi-decent shape for new papers, and he is not impressed.

ALLISON. Dagwood, I mean Mr. Bumstead?

MARGARET. No, Mr. Drewry. He doesn't like the ideas or the numbers. He's upset. Bumstead isn't happy. And after that disaster of a meeting disbands, I find an apple on my desk. I assume from Ethan. I don't know whether to feel like a first-grade teacher or Snow White. Bumstead comes in and wants copies of all my files and accounts from the last six months. I'm being reviewed. Let's see . . . I spill hot coffee in my lap at 3. 42 p.m. Not a pleasant feeling. My, well, everything between my navel and my knees should be sufficiently blistered by now. My secretary quits at 3. 55. She and her boyfriend evidently fought over the phone—while she is on the clock no less—and he's left for California. She leaves in an uproar.

ALLISON. She has worked for you for years.

MARGARET. Yep. And Bumstead sees her leave. I can only guess what he assumed. I get to the car. It won't start. I have to call the station to get a boost. I get home. Remember where the cancer sticks are, light one, take a major puff, savor the moment, drop the ashtray, which explodes into a million pieces. I drop the cigarette, which burns a hole in the carpet.

ALLISON. No.

MARGARET. Yes. I clean it up, and you walked in.

ALLISON. Sorry to spoil all your fun.

MARGARET. 's all right. You can't live your life in an amusement park.

ALLISON.   I have heard of people doing that.

MARGARET. You're insane.

ALLISON.   Not too bad.

MARGARET. I'm going that way.

ALLISON.   That's just unreal. That's a horrible day.

MARGARET.   I told you. Things cannot get worse.

There is a knock at the door.

ALLISON.   Talk about dramatic timing. Do you want me to get that? Or do you want to take a chance at making your day even more exciting?

MARGARET. Aw. Let me answer it. It just adds to the fun.

ALLISON.   Have at it.

MARGARET rises and goes to the door. Before she answers it, she turns and grins at ALLISON.

MARGARET. Carpe diem. *(She opens the door wide with great force.)*

Standing in the door is a lady approximately 65 years of age. She is dressed in expensive clothes, wears expensive jewelry, and has the air of an aristocrat.

SADIE. Good afternoon, dear.

MARGARET. *(Stands silent for a moment, mouth ajar, turns methodically to ALLISON and speaks)* Allison, *dear,* it's Aunt Sadie-Lady.

ALLISON.   *(Excitedly)* Aunt Sadie! No, it can't be you. *(She hops up and runs to the door.)*

SADIE.   It can, and it is.

MARGARET. *(Less than excite.)* It is.

SADIE.   Allison, how nice to see you, dear.

ALLISON.   What a surprise! *(She hugs Sadie.)*

MARGARET. Yes. What a surprise.

SADIE.   And don't I merit a hug from you, Margaret?

MARGARET. Of course, you do, Aunt Sadie-Lady. *(She hugs Sadie.)* It was just a surprise to see you. It's been a long time.

SADIE.   Not too long. Just a few months.

MARGARET. Oh, just a few months. It's seemed much longer.

SADIE.   Look. I know that what I said at Christmas was uncalled for. I have thought it
              out, and I am capable of being wrong and jumping to conclusions. There. I said
              it.

MARGARET. Hmm. She admits she shouldn't have said the first thing that came to her mind.
              I'm impressed.

SADIE.   Look, dear. It's an apology. It doesn't come easily for me, not at all.

ALLISON.   Margaret?

MARGARET. All right. All right. Apology accepted. Just come in. You're letting the climate-
              controlled air out.

ALLISON.   Yes, come in, Aunt Sadie.

SADIE.   Thank you, dears. *(She grabs a small bag and looks down at her other bags as if
              she is anticipating ALLISON and MARGARET to bring them inside. They oblige
              and bring the bags in. After they have put them down, SADIE takes her first step
              inside. Behind her, a young man wearing dark glasses is standing. ALLISON and
              MARGARET are somewhat startled.)*

ALLISON.   Aunt Sadie! There's a . . . a . . . young man behind you.

SADIE.   Oh, yes. I forgot to tell you.

MARGARET. Look, I can carry a reasonably-sized bag, but I have to draw the line somewhere.

SADIE.   Allison, Margaret, this is Spartan.

MARGARET. Spartan?

SPARTAN.   *(He grins and holds out his hand as if to accept a handshake.)* Good day, ladies.

ALLISON.   *(Approaching first.)* Spartan. It's nice to meet you. *(She shakes his hand.)*

SPARTAN.   *(Kisses her hand unexpectedly.)* Charmed. You must be Allison.

ALLISON.   *(Grins and answers nervously.)* Why, thank you, Mr. Spartan.

SPARTAN.   Spartan. Just plain Spartan.

18

ALLISON.   Margaret, this is Spartan.

He holds his hand out again.

SPARTAN.   And Margaret, it is a pleasure to meet you as well.

MARGARET.   *(Much less eager. She shakes his hand.)* Spartan.

ALLISON.   Come in. Come in, Spartan.

He enters slowly.

SADIE.   Allison, Margaret, I hope you don't mind my bringing Spartan with me. I didn't know how you would take to a guest you have not yet met, but I took a chance. He's such a nice young man. I didn't want to have him just sit in the car.

MARGARET. May I ask who he is?

SADIE pulls them aside.

ALLISON.   Is he a new *friend*, Aunt Sadie?

SADIE.   Heavens no. *(Laughs.)* I just picked him up about an hour ago.

MARGARET. Picked him up?

SADIE.   Yes, he was walking on the side of the highway.

MARGARET. A hitchhiker?

ALLISON.   A hitchhiker?

SADIE.   A crude term.

MARGARET. Are you nuts?

ALLISON.   Aunt Sadie, don't you know how dangerous that is?

SADIE.   I don't need a lecture, girls.

MARGARET. No, you need a brain. You just can't pick up people off the side of the roads these days.

ALLISON.   It's very dangerous. You could have been killed.

MARGARET. He could be a killer.

SADIE. Look at him, girls. He's harmless. He's kind and sweet, and he is . . . just . . . blind.

MARGARET. Okay. A killer you could dodge, but a possible killer nonetheless.

ALLISON. Aunt Sadie, you just have to be careful these days.

SADIE. I'm aware of that. I haven't made to my wise years without knowing that. *(To Margaret)* No comment, thank you. But there was something about him that made me pick him up.

ALLISON. ESP?

MARGARET. LSD?

SADIE. TLC. Tender loving care. *(MARGARET laughs.)* Yes, TLC. He looked so sweet and helpless.

MARGARET. You have never been one to be overly compassionate, Aunt Sadie-Lady.

SADIE. Who gave you this house? *(MARGARET looks down.)* Who, not having one child of her own, wanted to give to her two nieces, the daughters of my dear departed sisters, something to help them?

ALLISON. We know, Aunt Sadie. We know you love us, but you *know us*. This is a stranger.

SADIE. And who better to show compassion to? You can't be a Good Samaritan to an aristocrat.

SPARTAN. I can assure you, Allison, Margaret, that I am no killer.

ALLISON. Excellent hearing.

MARGARET. And he already knows our names well?

SADIE. We have been talking the last hour. Wonderful conversation.

MARGARET. And you told him about us?

SADIE. Well, I *was* coming to visit the two of you.

ALLISON. Well, have a seat, Spartan. Make yourself at home. *(He hesitates.)* Of course, I am sorry. You can't . . . *(She stops, embarrassed.)*

20

SPARTAN. No, I can't see. That's okay, Allison. I know I'm blind.

SADIE. Isn't he charming?

MARGARET. *(Sarcastically)* Simply irresistible.

SADIE. Behave, Margaret.

MARGARET. Yes'm.

SPARTAN. *(Sitting)* So, Allison, Margaret, Sadie told me all about you.

MARGARET. Oh, she did?

SPARTAN. Oh, I am sure not *all* about you. Just the good stuff.

SADIE. It was a short drive.

ALLISON. Aunt Sadie!

SADIE. Just joking, dear. You were at least three-forths of the conversation.

MARGARET. It's nice to know that I am loved.

SPARTAN. Oh, you are, Margaret. You are. More than you realize. More than your aunt
even realizes.

SADIE. Pardon me?

SPARTAN. Margaret, I know it may seem that the two of you don't see eye-to-eye, but it's
only because you are so much alike.

MARGARET. Pardon me?

ALLISON. You're so right, Spartan. I've said that for years.

SADIE. Pardon me?

ALLISON. Aunt Sadie, I've known that for years, but you two won't see it. You can't.
You're blind to it. *(To Spartan.)* Sorry.

SPARTAN. No offense taken.

MARGARET. I need a cigarette.

SADIE.   I thought you quit.

MARGARET. Addiction is heredity. Blood is thicker than patches.

ALLISON.   Wow, you're good, Spartan! After just watching, well, listening, to the two of
               them, you figured them out.

SPARTAN.   I'm good with people.

MARGARET. Evidently.

SADIE.   Watch it, Margaret. Your wit is exposed.

ALLISON.   Where are you headed, Spartan?

MARGARET. Why did you bring him in?

ALLISON and SADIE. Margaret?!

MARGARET. No offense, Spartan. It's just unusual to bring a hitchhiker to a home. The usual
               procedure, if I'm not mistaken, is to provide a ride, and say, "Well, this is the end
               of the road for me. Good luck, sir."

SADIE.   He's not your ordinary young man, Margaret. He is not your "usual" hitchhiker
               type. He and I got along well, and I thought maybe we could offer him something
               to eat. He's on a long journey.

MARGARET. It just gets stranger.

ALLISON.   It's just been an odd day, Aunt Sadie.

SPARTAN.   How big is your aquarium, ladies?

MARGARET. How do you know we have an aquarium?

SPARTAN.   I'm blind, but I'm not deaf. I can hear it.

ALLISON.   I've heard that with the loss of one sense, the others get stronger. Is that true?

SPARTAN.   Yes. Many senses are keener.

ALLISON.   Really?

SPARTAN.   More than you could imagine.

MARGARET. I need a cigarette.

SADIE.   I thought you quit.

MARGARET. We've had this conversation.

SPARTAN.   How big is it?

MARGARET. What?

SPARTAN.   Your aquarium, the fish tank.

ALLISON.   How many gallons is it, Margaret?

MARGARET. Beats me. A lot.

SADIE.   Such accuracy.

SPARTAN.   I can smell it, too.

ALLISON.   The aquarium?

SPARTAN.   Yes. It's a little stale. It's been a while since you changed the water, hasn't it?

ALLISON.   I don't know. When did we last change the water in the tank, Margaret?

MARGARET. Aunt Sadie-Lady, I thought your guest was hungry. You think we should prepare him a snack for the road?

SPARTAN.   *(Standing.)* I can take a hint. I'll be leaving now.

ALLISON.   No. Don't go. Margaret, do behave. Spartan is our guest. *(To Spartan again)* Please sit down, Spartan. We'll get you something to eat. *(He sits.)*

SADIE.   I'll get him something. *(Standing)* Is the kitchen where it was when I gave it to you?

MARGARET. We thought about moving it next to the pool, but we got lazy.

SADIE.   Imagine that. Please be nice to our guest, ladies. *(She exits to the kitchen.)*

ALLISON.   Well, Spartan, where are you from?

SPARTAN.   Nowhere really.

MARGARET. Figures.

ALLISON.   Margaret, behave, please.

SPARTAN.   Don't worry about it. I understand your sarcasm, Margaret. All of my life, I have
             lived in a cruel world, unaccepting of me.

ALLISON.   Aw. Don't you feel bad now, Margaret?

MARGARET. I need a cigarette.

ALLISON.   By all means, smoke, Margaret!

SPARTAN.   Your aunt seems to be a very nice lady.

ALLISON.   She is. She is. She is a little rough around the edges when it comes to her
             comments.

MARGARET. A little?

ALLISON.   A little. But it's nothing I'm not *very* used to.

SPARTAN.   I'll bet.

MARGARET. This is a conspiracy.

ALLISON.   Nothing is hidden, Margaret. We're right here.

SPARTAN.   Sadie was kind to have picked me up.

ALLISON.   She can be a kind lady.

SPARTAN.   I'm on a journey of sorts. My father was in the military, so there was no one
             place I could call home. I've lived all over the United States and many places in
             Europe and in the Pacific. Oh, the smell of the ocean on a warm summer
             morning!

ALLISON.   How sweet.

MARGARET. How tropical.

They both look at her.

SPARTAN.   As soon as my father earned his commission, we were on a commercial plane that
             was flying across the continental U.S. Needless to say, it crashed.

ALLISON.   No.

24

SPARTAN.   Yes. Both of my parents perished. I was the only survivor out of nearly 200 passengers.

ALLISON.   Oh, you poor baby!

SPARTAN.   It was hours before they found me.

MARGARET. Eating a diet of grubs and leaves.

ALLISON.   Margaret! What is wrong with you?

SPARTAN.   It's all right, Allison. She's just suspicious of others. It's understandable.

MARGARET. You saw through me. Darn.

ALLISON.   Forgive her, Spartan. She knows not what she does.

SPARTAN.   Don't worry about it.

ALLISON.   Continue. Please.

SPARTAN.   Oh, there's not much more to tell. I was an only child, so I've basically been alone ever since. I made up my mind that I'm not the type of person to live in one place, so I've been on the road, traveling from place to place, trying to visit all the areas I've not yet ventured into. I've danced on Ellis Island, sang at Mount Rushmore, drunk espresso in Seattle, felt the warmth of the San Diego sun, and yes, Margaret, I've eaten grubs in the forests of Appalachia.

ALLISON.   How wonderful!

MARGARET. Grubs? Wonderful? There are some in the yard, Allison, if you want to live the adventure.

ALLISON.   No. The varied experiences. How exciting. Especially for someone who . . . (*Pauses*)

SPARTAN.   Is blind. That's okay. I know I'm blind.

MARGARET. Who's the one with the foot-in-the-mouth disease now, Allison, dear?

SPARTAN.   It's all right. It really is.

MARGARET. I have to admit, though. You have done a lot. That is quite an impressive travel log.

SPARTAN.   Why, thank you, Margaret. A crack in the ice sculpture?

MARGARET. Better than in the fish tank.

SPARTAN. True.

ALLISON. Where are you headed now?

SPARTAN. I don't really know. That's the beauty of it all. I'm just going wherever I end up. Just traveling the road. I know I don't want to go where I've already been. I just hope to find a new place. *(Standing.)* I want to live the adventure. See, *(pauses)* well, hear, smell, taste, and feel the world. Looking for truth and contentment and love.

ALLISON. That is so inspirational! *(In a complete change of mood, she sounds motherly.)* Sit down before you trip over something. *(He turns her way and sits slowly.)*

MARGARET. Looking for love? Don't waste your time. It doesn't exist.

ALLISON. Don't be so cynical.

MARGARET. *(As if she didn't hear her)* When you think it's love, it's fraudulent, unreal. You give your heart away and think you have received one in return, but then it's just deception knocking on your door.

There is a knock on the door.

SPARTAN. Wow. I can hear it.

MARGARET. What now?

ALLISON. Let me get it this time.

MARGARET. No please. Let's not break a record.

MARGARET rushes to the door to beat ALLISON, who also makes her way there.

MARGARET. And what's behind Door Number One?

She flings open the door. Standing there are Cynthia and Marcus.

CYNTHIA and MARCUS. Ciao!

(MARGARET screams.)

ALLISON. Cynthia! Marcus! The, the, the surprise!

MARGARET. The nerve!

CYNTHIA. Hello, ladies!

MARCUS. How are you, Allison?

ALLISON. I am, um, fine, Marcus.

CYNTHIA. Allison. *(Takes her hand)*

ALLISON. *(Fearfully)* Cynthia. I thought you two were honeymooning in Italy.

MARCUS. Oh, you got the postcard?

MARGARET. Today.

MARCUS. *(Laughing)* The efficiency of the Italian postal service.

CYNTHIA. Yes, but everything else there is just perfect.

ALLISON. *(Attempting to change the subject)* Nice flight home?

CYNTHIA. It was okay.

MARCUS. Margaret, you should see Italy! It's gorgeous. You should see it.

MARGARET. I've wanted to for years, Marcus. You know that.

CYNTHIA. It's the perfect place to honeymoon. It's so romantic.

ALLISON. *(Attempting to change the subject)* No rain at JFK?

MARGARET. I don't need to hear this.

MARCUS. What's wrong, Margaret?

MARGARET. What's wrong? What's wrong? You have the audacity to ask me what's wrong?

CYNTHIA. You need to calm down. We were being nice by coming by. Do you know how difficult it is to visit the home of my new husband's ex-fiancée? I think it's an extremely noble gesture on my part.

MARGARET. Noble?

CYNTHIA. Look, we're not kids here. I know that you and Marcus were close. And that doesn't just disappear. He told me that you two had decided to remain friends, and I'm okay with that, but not at the expense of listening to vile, sarcastic remarks.

MARGARET. I don't believe this. I'm here in my house. I'm living the day from hell. All my life I have dreamed of visiting Italy, and then I get word that the man I loved more than life itself is taking his new bride there. *Then,* they show up at my house, and I'm unreasonable to be upset?

MARCUS. Margaret. Wait a minute now.

SPARTAN. She's right.

CYNTHIA. What?

MARCUS. Who are you?

SPARTAN. *(Standing and outstretching his arm for a handshake.)* I'm Spartan.

MARCUS shakes his hand.

MARCUS. Spartan?

CYNTHIA. What kind of name is that?

MARCUS, SPARTAN, ALLISON, and MARGARET.   Greek.

CYNTHIA. Oh.

SPARTAN. She's right. She's crude, bitter, and sarcastic, but she's right in this matter.

CYNTHIA. Wait a minute.

SPARTAN. She has a right to be upset. She's hurt. Not only has the one she loves rejected her, . . .

MARGARET. *(Sarcastically)* Thanks.

SPARTAN. You're welcome. . . . but he arrives on her turf with his new choice and has recently arrived from the place she has always wanted to visit. It's like rubbing it in her face.

MARGARET. *(Sincerely)* Thanks.

SPARTAN. You're welcome.

CYNTHIA. Wait a minute. I don't have to listen to a blind weirdo tell me what to do.

28

MARGARET. Watch your mouth. Don't you dare call him a weirdo! There is only one weirdo here.

There is a knock at the door.

ALLISON.   No.

MARGARET. Why not? *(Going to the door)*

CYNTHIA.   I have never!!

MARGARET. Don't kid yourself. You do all the time.

MARCUS.   Margaret, I can't stand here and allow you to insult my wife.

MARGARET. Okay. Don't stand there then.

There is a knock at the door again.

ETHAN's voice. Margaret, is that you?

MARGARET.   No!

ALLISON.   Who is it?

MARGARET. No!

ALLISON.   Who is it?

MARGARET. Ethan Plumber.

ALLISON.   No!

SPARTAN.   Who's Ethan?

MARGARET and ALLISON. The nerd boy.

ALLISON.   *(Finishing the sentence)* . . . who's in love with Margaret.

MARGARET.   Let's not answer it.

ALLISON. You have to answer it. He's already heard us. You shouldn't have borrowed that money from him.

SPARTAN.   You borrowed money from a nerd who's in love with you?

MARCUS.   Margaret, that was not a good idea.

MARGARET. I know! I know!

ETHAN's voice. Margaret, open the door. I want to talk to you.

MARGARET. I have to hide. Allison, help me.

SPARTAN.   Is it that bad?

MARGARET and ALLISON. Yes.

MARGARET. I'm going to the bedroom. Get rid of him. *(She walks off-stage.)*

ALLISON.   Okay.

CYNTHIA.   *(Going to the door)* This is ridiculous. I'll answer it.

ALLISON.   *(Intercepting)* Oh, no you don't. Back off, sister. *(ALLISON answers the door.)* Ethan, how nice to see you again.

ETHAN.   *(He is dressed very strangely, like a typical nerd or a very, very odd individual.)* Hello, Allison. Where's Margaret? I'm here to see her. Where is she?

ALLISON.   She's not here, Ethan.

ETHAN.   *(Snorting)* I just heard her, Allison. She's here. She's just playing hard to get.

ALLISON.   No, Ethan. That's not it.

ETHAN.   *(Coming in uninvited)* Who are all these people? Are all of you here to see Margaret?

CYNTHIA.   No.

ETHAN.   Good. 'Cause she's mine. I have been trying to get her for seven years, three months, and ten days.

SPARTAN.   Oh, my.

ETHAN.   *(Paranoid)* What are you looking at?

SPARTAN.   Nothing.

ETHAN.   Good.

ALLISON.   That's just rude.

SPARTAN.   It's all right.

ALLISON.   No, it's not.

ETHAN.   Where's Margaret?

MARCUS.   Why do you want to know?

CYNTHIA.   *(To Marcus)* Why do you ask?

MARCUS.   There's no need of this.

ALLISON.   No, there's not.

ETHAN.   For seven years, three months, and . . .

SPARTAN.   . . . ten days. We heard you.

ETHAN.   Watch it, blind boy.

MARCUS.   Pick on someone with your own sight.

SPARTAN.   Thanks, Marcus. But I can handle him.

MARCUS.   Okay. Just helping.

CYNTHIA.   What's going on here?

ALLISON.   Shut up.

CYNTHIA.   What?!

ALLISON, MARCUS, and SPARTAN.   Shut up.

CYNTHIA sits down angrily.

ETHAN.   Margaret proved today that she needs me. She borrowed some cash from me today so that she could pay for lunch. It's a sign. She planned it.

ALLISON.   She *lost* her wallet earlier, Ethan! She had no choice.

ETHAN.   Likely story. It was a plan. She was trying to make a connection with me.

MARCUS.   You're insane. She has better taste than to choose you!

ETHAN.   And I suppose that she would choose you.

MARCUS.   Yes, she did.

CYNTHIA.   *(Standing)* I'm leaving. I'm not listening to this! *(She storms out.)*

Everyone remains still. Then they continue as if she were never there.

ETHAN.   She wants me as much as I want her.

SPARTAN.   Are you for real?

ETHAN.   Let's take it outside, blind boy!

SPARTAN.   That's it! *(Holding up his fists)*

ALLISON.   Wait a minute! This is ridiculous! Ethan, I know that you've liked Margaret for a long time.

ETHAN.   Seven years . . .

ALLISON.   We know! But she doesn't feel the same way, Ethan. She's not interested in you in that way!

ETHAN.   She orchestrated a way to borrow money from me.

ALLISON.   She lost her wallet, Ethan.

ETHAN.   Likely story.

ALLISON.   She lost her wallet! It was a hard day! Losing her wallet was one of about 1000 things that went wrong today, Ethan. She doesn't need this, too.

ETHAN.   Are you trying to tell me something?

ALLISON.   She doesn't like you that way, Ethan!

ETHAN.   But she borrowed money from me. She talked to me and borrowed money from me.

ALLISON.   You were the only person in the deli she knew. She bought her food, realized her wallet was gone, and had to find someone to help.

ETHAN.   Our new boss, Bumstead, was there.

ALLISON.   She couldn't ask him.

ETHAN.   Why not. Is *he* in love with her?

There is a knock at the door.

SPARTAN.   You gotta be kidding.

SADIE.   *(Entering with a plate of food)* What's going on in here?

MARCUS.   Sadie.

SADIE.   Marcus, what are you doing here?

There is a knock at the door again.

MARCUS.   Just visiting.

SADIE.   Does anyone hear the door? *(She hands the plate to SPARTAN.)* Here, Spartan.

SPARTAN.   Thanks.

ALLISON.   Aunt Sadie, I need to sit down.

SADIE.   *(To ETHAN)* Who are you?

ETHAN.   I'm Ethan Plumber, Aunt Sadie.

SADIE.   I am not your aunt.

There is a very loud knock at the door.

SPARTAN.   Good grubs.

SADIE.   Must I answer the door? *(She goes to the door and answers it. Standing at the entrance is SHERWOOD BUMSTEAD. He is a nice-looking, thirty-to-forty-year-old man, dressed in business attire.)* May I help you?

BUMSTEAD. Yes, my name is Sherwood Bumstead.

SADIE.   Right. Sure, it is. I'm in no mood for pranks, young man. *(She starts to close the door, but he leans in.)*

BUMSTEAD. No, really, my name is Sherwood Bumstead, and I'm here to see Margaret. I'm her new boss.

ALLISON.   Bumstead?

ETHAN.   Mr. Bumstead?

BUMSTEAD. Plumber? What are you doing here?

ETHAN.   You love her, don't you? One day, and she has you under her spell. I knew it.

BUMSTEAD. Pardon me?

SADIE.   You're here to see Margaret?

BUMSTEAD. If I may.

SADIE.   Well most certainly you can. You are mannerly. That goes a long way.

ETHAN.   She's not home.

SADIE.   Don't be ridiculous. I just saw her. She slipped into her bedroom a few minutes
              ago. *(She goes to find MARGARET.)*

ETHAN.   You lied to me.

ALLISON.   Yes, we did. Okay. We lied. She doesn't want to see you!

ETHAN.   I have a feeling that you are trying to tell me something.

SPARTAN.   All at once I don't feel so blind.

ETHAN.   I love her.

BUMSTEAD. Plumber, there's a policy about romance at work. I can't have that.

ETHAN.   Um. I ... um... I can't help it. She is my life. I love her.

BUMSTEAD. Well, if that be the case, you need to find another place to work.

ETHAN.   I can't. I, um, I, it took me five years to find a place that wanted to hire me.
              Nowhere else understood my genius. I need this job. I don't want to leave.

BUMSTEAD. Well, I think you need to control your feelings, then.

ETHAN.   But, Mr. Bumstead, for seven years . . .

BUMSTEAD. Times change, Plumber. Get over it. In fact, if I hear of you making so much as one flirtatious comment or one unwelcome glance at Ms. Meadows, I'll dismiss you myself.

ETHAN. But, Mr. Bumstead . . .

BUMSTEAD. Myself.

ETHAN. But she borrowed six dollars and eighty-four cents from me at lunch today, and I thought . . .

BUMSTEAD. *(Pulling out his wallet)* $6.84? Okay, Plumber, here's a ten. Keep the change. Forget about it all.

ETHAN. But at lunch . . .

BUMSTEAD. Take the money and go home, Plumber. Or do want to spend five more years looking for a boss willing to put up with you?

ETHAN. *(Reluctantly taking the money)* Go home?

BUMSTEAD. Go home.

ETHAN. Yes, sir. *(He starts to leave.)* Nice fish tank.

ALLISON. Thanks.

ETHAN leaves.

ALLISON. Thank you, Mr. Bumstead.

BUMSTEAD. No problem. I really need to see Margaret. Is she coming?

ALLISON. I'll go see what's keeping her. *(She goes toward the bedroom.)*

There is a little awkward silence.

BUMSTEAD. *(To Marcus)* Sherwood Bumstead.

MARCUS. Marcus Reelus.

BUMSTEAD. *(To Spartan)* Sherwood Bumstead.

SPARTAN. *(Sticking his hand out for BUMSTEAD to grab)* Spartan.

BUMSTEAD. Spartan . . .? *(Anticipating a last name)*

SPARTAN. Just Spartan. Just traveling through. Sightseeing.

There are a few moments of awkward silence again.

BUMSTEAD. Well, nice aquarium.

MARCUS. Yep. Been there for as long as I've known the girls.

SPARTAN. Same here.

BUMSTEAD. It's a pretty nice one. All these fish in a tank swimming around for everyone to see. Out of their natural habitats. It's interesting to see how they react to all the stimuli they're exposed to. Unnatural conditions. And yet they survive. It becomes real for them.

SPARTAN. The water is stale, though.

BUMSTEAD. You think so?

SPARTAN. I know so. I can smell it.

BUMSTEAD. Maybe you just need to change the water every once in a while to keep it from getting boring.

SPARTAN and MARCUS. Maybe so.

MARGARET, ALLISON, and SADIE re-enter.

MARGARET. Mr. Bumstead.

BUMSTEAD. Margaret. *(Correcting himself)* Well, Ms. Meadows.

MARGARET. "Margaret" is fine.

MARCUS. Yes, she is.

SADIE. Hush.

MARGARET. *(To Marcus)* You're still here?

BUMSTEAD. I wanted to stop by . . . *(Hesitates)*

MARGARET. Mr. Bumstead, I am really sorry about the Drewry account. I promise that I'm a much better presenter than I was today.

BUMSTEAD. I know.

MARGARET. Pardon?

BUMSTEAD. I know you are. Look, I owe you an apology. I have examined all the paperwork I took home with me, and frankly, I'm impressed.

MARGARET. You are?

SADIE. You are?

ALLISON. He is.

BUMSTEAD. I am. You're an excellent organizer and a major asset to our company. I really jumped to conclusions today. I was out of sorts myself, and I had been told about this hotshot junior executive that was dynamite in a dress, or in whatever you choose to wear. I was just looking for problems I guess. What I found was sound skills and a good worker. I was wrong.

MARGARET. Wow. I'm not used to apologies—or anything like this.

SADIE. Or to giving them either.

ALLISON. That's so nice, Mr. Bumstead.

MARGARET. Did you meet my cousin, Allison Bailey?

BUMSTEAD. In passing. *(To Allison)* Ms. Bailey.

ALLISON. Mr. Bumstead.

BUMSTEAD. Call me "Sherwood."

ALLISON. Sherwood.

MARGARET. I appreciate your coming, Mr. Bumstead.

BUMSTEAD. Please call me "Sherwood" as well, Ms. Meadows.

MARGARET. Call me "Margaret," "Sherwood as well." *(They laugh. Obviously, there is a connection between them.)*

SADIE. I think I'm going to be sick.

ALLISON. There's antacid in the kitchen.

37

SADIE.   It's all gone.

SPARTAN.   I've enjoyed the afternoon fun, but I guess I need to hit the road again. *(He rises.)*

ALLISON.   Don't go.

SADIE.   Stay awhile.

SPARTAN.   I have places to go, people to . . . well, people to be around.

MARGARET. Aw, hang around a while, Spartan. The excitement's starting to wear down.

(There is a knock at the door.)

SPARTAN.   Okay. I'll stay. I gotta see this. . . figuratively speaking.

(MARGARET goes to the door and opens it. MILDRED, her secretary, is there, crying.)

MARGARET. Mildred, what are you doing here? You're supposed to be in California.

MILDRED.   I'm sorry, Ms. Meadows. I hate to bother you at home, but I need to beg you to let me come back.

MARGARET. What's wrong, Mildred?

MILDRED.   *(She enters.)* Roger has another woman. I got to the airport, but before I was to board the plane, I called and checked my messages on my voice mail at home. And there was. . . *(Weeping)* Roger and his woman telling me about their love. It was more than I could take.

MARGARET. I'm sorry, Mildred.

MILDRED.   Then I got mad!!! *(All stand back.)* I mean, the nerve. I give my heart to him, and he rips it out when he finds a replacement.

MARCUS.   I think I need to go.

MARGARET. Why are you in such a hurry, Romeo?

MARCUS.   Well, my wife did leave highly upset a while back. I need to see if she is okay.

MILDRED.   *(To Marcus)* You did the same thing, didn't you?

MARCUS.   I really have to go. Bye. *(He starts to leave.)*

SADIE.   Have a nice life, Marcus.

38

ALLISON.   Feel free to stop by for dinner sometime.

MARCUS leaves in a hurry.

MARGARET.   I'm sorry, Mildred. Of course, you can come back . . . if Sherwood, um, Mr. Bumstead agrees. Is that okay, Sherwood?

MILDRED.   *(Just now noticing him)* Oh, Mr. Bumstead, I didn't know you were here. I hope I didn't interrupt anything.

BUMSTEAD. Of course not. And you can come back. I have to admit that I did wonder why you left in a flurry today.

MILDRED.   And Ms. Meadows is a great worker and a pleasure to work for.

BUMSTEAD. I know, Mildred.

MILDRED.   And I am the one who accidentally threw away the Drewry papers. She worked on those for weeks. It was all my fault.

BUMSTEAD. Don't worry about it, Mildred. I know that Ms. Meadows is a wonderful accountant and salesperson. Drewry was an idiot to turn her down.

MARGARET. Really? *(Sweetly)* You think that?

BUMSTEAD. Yes.

SADIE.   I need a cigarette.

ALLISON.   You don't smoke.

SADIE.   I forgot.

BUMSTEAD. Go home, Mildred.

MILDRED.   Sir?

BUMSTEAD. Go home. You need sleep. Be at work bright and early in the morning ready to assist a soon-to-be senior salesperson.

MARGARET. Sherwood!

BUMSTEAD. Go home, Mildred.

MILDRED.   *(Confused)* Yes, sir. *(She leaves.)*

SPARTAN.   You are all such subtle people.

SADIE.   We try.

ALLISON.   Spartan, stay a while. I'm interested in chatting some more tonight. How's that for subtly?

SPARTAN.   I need a cigarette. *(Laughing)*

BUMSTEAD. I guess I need to go, too. I came to apologize and make things right.

MARGARET. You don't have to go.

BUMSTEAD. I don't?

MARGARET. No. Stay for dinner.

BUMSTEAD. Dinner?

ALLISON.   Yes, you, too, Spartan. Stay for dinner.

BUMSTEAD. I will if he will.

SPARTAN.   I see how you are. *(Laughing)* Well, not literally.

ALLISON.   Stay.

MARGARET. Yes, stay.

ALLISON.   It's not often she's in such a good mood. Stay. Carpe diem.

SPARTAN.   Sure. I have no plans.

BUMSTEAD. Sure. I can be late for work.

SADIE.   Who's cooking dinner?

MARGARET and ALLISON. You are.

SADIE.   The gratitude. *(She walks toward the kitchen.)*

They two couples follow, holding hands.

BUMSTEAD. *(To SPARTAN—as they are all leaving stage)* Are you looking for a job?

40

SPARTAN.   I might be, if it were exciting enough.

BUMSTEAD. I need to hire a photographer. Interested?

MARGARET. Sherwood!

SPARTAN.   Maybe. We'll see.

They exit.

*A **strongly** suggested directorial choice: SPARTAN, as he is leaving, should pull down his glasses and wink at the audience, revealing that he is not in fact blind.*

Lowery Christopher Collins (Chris) has been an educator and writer for over thirty years. He is currently a professor of English at Panola College in Carthage, Texas. He has taught at the high school, middle school, and elementary school levels and as an English and literature instructor at the college and university level. For several years, he was a high school theatre director and a gifted education consultant. He's been honored with several teaching awards, including the Young Audiences of Northeast Texas Outstanding Service to the Profession Award and the Kennedy Center's Steven Sondheim Award for being one of the most "Inspirational Teachers" in the U.S.

He is also an award-winning playwright of over thirty scripts, a weekly newspaper columnist, a short story writer, a poet, a pianist, a vocalist, a songwriter, a recording artist with Daywind Studios, the founder and artistic director of Stagelands Theatre Company, an aspiring novelist, and a (former) choir director. He's taught a variety of classes, from rhetoric and composition to literature to acting to the Bible.

He holds a Bachelor of Arts Degree in English and History and a Master of Arts Degree in English from Stephen F. Austin State University in Texas and has served on fine arts and gifted education committees as well as on a board of governors for a small playhouse.

In addition to his interests in teaching, directing, and writing, he has a fondness for lighthouses, windmills, filmmaking, salsa, sculpture, Flannery O'Connor, travel, dominos, guacamole, social media, genetics, Maine, landscaping, pillows, gospel music, Shakespeare, marbles, YouTube, quantum physics, movies, weird jokes, maps, trees, cold rooms, and Texas.

 He can be reached at mrchriscollins@hotmail.com,

on Facebook at www.facebook.com/tofferdreams,

on Twitter at "tofferdreams,"

and at his website: www.ChristopherCollinsOnline.com.

To view Christopher Collins's books and other writing, visit Ponderlake Publishing, at www.ponderlake.com.